A SILENT ECHO

A FIGHT FOR A LIFE

JOJO D'SOUZA

Made with ♥ on the Notion Press Platform
www.notionpress.com

To Suzan

My partner, friend, and wife, the centre of our lives. Your unwavering fight against all odds to bring our unborn child into this world has taught us the true meaning of strength and resilience. Your love and determination have been our guiding light.

Suzan and Ravi, as their journey begins

To my sons, Shaun and Shane, for being unwavering pillars of support. From the moment we faced the heart-wrenching choice between saving Mumma Suzan's life and hoping for a miracle, your strength and love have united us.

Your prayers and steadfast belief have shown us the power of faith and family.

To the Doctors, Priests, Friends and for all the countless prayers that were offered for us with grace, and that gave us solace during our most difficult times. Your compassion and dedication have been our lifeline.

With deep gratitude and love.
- Ravi

Contents

Life has a way of weaving stories that we could never have imagined, and sometimes, those stories become the heartbeats of our lives. I met Ravi many years ago when we were both students at Regina Mundi High School in Goa. We shared the carefree days of youth, bound by friendship and the simple joys of growing up in the vibrant town of Vasco-da-Gama. Little did we know then that our paths would cross again in such profound ways, and that I would have the honour of telling the story of his incredible family.

Years passed, and as life took us in different directions, Ravi's journey led him to the high seas, working tirelessly as a chef on container ships along the American coast. His dedication to his family and his unwavering determination were traits that stood out even back in our school days. Meanwhile, my own path took me into the world of storytelling, acting, and filmmaking.

Our lives converged once more when Ravi met me and spoke about his sons and their dreams. It was then that our old friendship was rekindled, and I found myself drawn into the remarkable story of Ravi, his wife Suzan, and their sons. Their resilience, love, and faith in the face of adversity were both inspiring and humbling.

"A Silent Echo" is not just a book; it is a testament to the strength of the human spirit, the power of family, and the unyielding hope that carries us through the darkest of times. Suzan's journey, in particular, is a tale of immense courage. Faced with the challenges of a high-risk pregnancy and the loss of a child, she exemplifies the boundless love and sacrifice of a mother.

Ravi, the steadfast pillar of his family, navigated stormy seas both literally and metaphorically. His love for his family, his ability to remain strong despite the distances and hardships, and his determination to provide for them are woven into every chapter of this story.

Shane and Shaun, growing up too fast, took on responsibilities with maturity beyond their years, proving that strength often comes in the smallest packages.

As their family friend and author of this book, it has been a privilege to witness and document their journey. "A Silent Echo" is a tribute to their enduring spirit, and it serves as a reminder that even in the silence, there is a powerful echo of love, hope, and resilience.

May this story inspire you, as it has inspired me, to cherish every moment, to find strength in adversity, and to always listen for the silent echoes of the heart.

—
JOJO D'SOUZA
Writer, Dreamer and Creative Head at
Big Banner Entertainment and Media LLP, Goa

ᐳᐳᐳ

Preface

A few years of intense interactions with my friend Ravi, is what inspired the writing of this book in as much detail as possible, being true to the life and journey of the family as they dealt with the trauma of their child being declared - STILL BORN.

- **Suzan Fernandes, Mother/Wife.** Suzan is a resilient, loving mother with a strong faith and unwavering belief in miracles. She is determined and hopeful, despite the numerous medical setbacks during her pregnancy. Her strength lies in her emotional depth and the fierce love she has for her family. She is compassionate, determined, nurturing, and emotionally strong.
- **Ravi Fernandes, Father/Husband.** Ravi is a devoted husband and father, working as a seaman, which often keeps him away from home. He struggles with the physical distance from his family but remains emotionally connected and supportive. He is wise and street smart.
- **Shaun Fernandes, Elder Son.** Shaun is an early teenager who is mature beyond his years, bearing the weight of responsibility during his father's absence. He is deeply caring towards his mother and siblings and tries to stay strong for them. He loves music and creativity in all forms.
- **Shane Fernandes, Younger Son.** Shane is the more playful and carefree of the two brothers but is deeply affected by his mother's condition. He looks up to Shaun and tries to emulate his strength. He loves to travel, cook and is a foodie as well.

ᐅᐅᐅ

- ***Lisa, Family Friend.*** Lisa is a close friend to Suzan. She has always been there for the Fernandes family. She is a source of support and comfort, providing a steady presence during their trials.
- ***Dr. Gerrad, Lead Doctor.*** Dr. Gerrad is a seasoned obstetrician with a pragmatic approach to medicine. He is dedicated to his profession but often struggles with the emotional aspects of his job. He is a friend of the Fernandes Family.
- ***Dr. Sunita, Assistant Doctor.*** Dr. Sunita works closely with Dr. Gerrad and is known for her empathetic approach towards patients. She balances her medical expertise with a deep sense of compassion. She is diligent, patient, and warm-hearted.

ᐅᐅᐅ

"While the narrations in this book are true, some names and identifying details have been changed to protect the privacy of the people involved."

Prologue

It was a warm August night in 2007 when the Fernandes family found themselves facing their greatest challenge. Suzan, her heart swollen with both fear and fierce determination, lay in a sterile room, clutching the fragile thread of faith that bound her to her unborn child.

Outside, her sons Shane and Shaun played a game of 'chase', their innocent laughter a dark contrast to the painful struggles unfolding within. Ravi, thousands of miles away on a ship sailing through the indifferent ocean, felt the distance keenly. The sea, once a symbol of his adventures and livelihood, now seemed like a barrier, separating him from his family in their time of greatest need. His heart echoed with silent prayers, each wave a whisper of hope that his wife and unborn child would be safe.

> *"In the heart of this silence, a mother's love would resonate louder than any monitor, a father's prayers would span oceans, and the bond between brothers – Shaun and Shane would shine brightest in their darkest hour."*

ϷϷϷ

In a dimly lit room, a lone candle flickers, casting shadows on the walls. Suzan Fernandes sits by the window, her eyes closed, hands folded in prayer. The faint sound of a heartbeat monitor beeps rhythmically in the background. She whispers a prayer, her voice barely audible.

"Sacred Heart of Jesus, I place my trust in you."

She opens her eyes, gazing at the photograph on her bedside table. It's a picture of her with her husband Ravi and their two sons, Shaun and Shane. Tears well up as she caresses the image, her heart heavy with a mix of hope and despair. Tonight, she needs a miracle.

"This is their story - A Silent Echo!"

ᐅᐅᐅ

1

Anchored by Family

MERCY HOSPITAL - NIGHT - 15 AUG 2007. Shane and Shaun were chasing each other in the parking lot, their laughter echoing through the night. A car passed by slowly, its headlights briefly illuminating the sign that read "MERCY HOSPITAL." An ambulance enters and parks nearby, its flashing-lights casting an eerie glow. Inside, in the busy corridors of Mercy Hospital, the flickering fluorescent lights cast a pale glow on the worn hospital floors, as if the very building was tired from witnessing the countless stories of life and loss within its walls. Lisa, a close friend of Suzan, looked out from a window towards the boys playing.

Lisa is a vibrant and compassionate woman in her early thirties, exuding an infectious energy that instantly uplifts those around her. Her striking eyes sparkle with warmth and intelligence, while her auburn hair, often tied back in a practical ponytail, frames her face in soft waves. Lisa's presence is comforting and reassuring, making her a cherished friend and confidante.

Outside of work, Lisa is dedicated to her friends, especially Suzan and her sons. She consistently makes time for them, offering support and encouragement during their most challenging times. Her loyalty and unwavering support have made her an integral part of Suzan's extended family. Known for her quick wit and infectious laughter, Lisa's presence brings joy and comfort to those around her. She enjoys reading and exploring the outdoors, often taking long hikes to clear her mind and find inspiration.

"Shane, Shaun. Come in. There's something I need to tell you," Lisa called out, her voice trembling slightly.

Just then, Shaun's cellphone buzzed. He pulled it out and saw his dad's name on the screen. [RAVI].

Ravi was a man of great strength and resolve, qualities that had served him well in his role as a chef and a seaman. He had spent countless nights navigating the stormy oceans and high seas along the American coast, driven by a singular purpose: his family. Every dish he prepared in the ship's galley, every navigational decision he made, was fuelled by his unwavering commitment to those he loved.

He had always been a man of ambition, striving to achieve something significant in life. Yet, his focus had never strayed from his family. They were his anchor, grounding him through the roughest storms. Ravi's thoughts often wandered to them during his long voyages, drawing strength from their love and support.

Ravi was an ex-student of Regina Mundi High School in Goa, a place that had instilled in him the values of hard work and perseverance. Growing up in Vasco-da-Gama, a bustling port town, he came from a large, close-knit family. The family's pride and joy was their famous restaurant, TIDES INN! - A beloved institution in the town. The restaurant, with its rich aromas of Goan cuisine and lively atmosphere, had been the backdrop to Ravi's formative years.

The lessons learned in the kitchen of TIDES INN, under the watchful eyes of his parents had shaped Ravi into the man he was today. He carried those lessons with him to every ship he worked on, infusing his culinary creations with the flavours of home and the spirit of his family's legacy

Ravi stood on the deck of the massive container ship, the turbulent ocean churning beneath his feet. The wind whipped through his bald head, and the salt spray clung to his rugged face. Despite the stormy weather, his eyes remained focused and determined. Each wave that crashed against the ship was a reminder of the challenges he faced, both at sea and at home.

He was walking about restlessly during his break and then managed to get a call through to his son Shaun, just as Lisa had called Shaun inside to discuss some matters. At a very young age, Shaun was already manning the ship at home. The family discussed everything together. After a few failed attempts, Ravi had finally got range to make a call and Shaun answered. Ravi had earlier been contacted by the Doctors with some grave but debatable news on Suzan's condition.

"Hello, Papa? Aunt Lisa just called us inside. She said there's something she has to tell us..."

"Shaun?" Ravi's voice was strained, almost frantic.

"Shaun, listen to me. I spoke to the Doctors there. Once again they're saying that the baby has no heartbeat. They say that the baby has not survived. I don't believe them. You go in and see. Those doctors simply create confusion and fear..."

Shaun's heart sank. "Yes, Papa. A few months ago too they said the same thing. No heartbeat and all. I don't know what's going on, Papa. I wish you were... Okay, never mind."

Out at sea, Ravi stood on the deck of the ship that he worked on, taking a deep breath as the sound of the sea and passing seagulls momentarily distracted him. The vast expanse of water seemed to mock his helplessness. He knew that his sons Shaun and Shane were his wife Suzan's pillars of strength and support when he was out at sea, working hard to make ends meet. Ravi knew that he was the anchor of the family, and yet he understood why Shaun could not complete his sentence.

"I'm sorry that I am not there, son. This was all so sudden and unexpected. I'm delayed here for another fifteen days at least. You're the man of the house now. Be strong."

"I'll call you again later, okay, Papa? I'm going inside. I'm scared, Papa," Shaun's voice quivered.

"God is watching over us, son. Everything will be fine. I'll say a prayer as well," Ravi reassured him, looking up at the sky as if seeking divine intervention.

His mind raced back to a few months earlier.

ᗡᗡᗡ

2

We Can't Lose You!

MERCY HOSPITAL - NIGHT - 16 AUG 2007. The sun rose, casting a warm glow over the hospital. Suzan was awake in tears on the hospital bed. Shane and Shaun were beside her, trying to comfort her. "Papa is right, Mumma. Don't believe these doctors. Dr. Gerrad says he will run some tests as well," Shaun said, his voice full of determination. "I don't want to lose this child, Shaun. At any cost, save your little brother or sister," Suzan pleaded. "And lose you? No, Mumma. You are everything to us. I prayed so hard for you both to be with us. I'm sure God will listen," Shaun replied, holding her hand tightly. Dr. Gerrad entered with Dr. Sunita and a team. "Suzan, we need to operate. There are a lot of complications and I'm sorry that Ravi is not here, but we risk losing your life and the child is non-responsive. There's no sign of life or a heartbeat." "Save my child. That is all that I ask of you," Suzan implored, her voice breaking.

Dr. Gerrad shook his head. "Speak to your husband before we proceed. Is there no one from your families available for you?" Suzan looked down in silence.

"Suzan and Ravi Fernandes spoke about the issue with their unborn child a few months before delivery. Suzan's side of the family did not offer much support at that time, but Ravi's family was occasionally at the hospital. There wasn't much anyone could do because they had decided to go through with what the doctors advised. To the Medical Staff, the child was already clinically dead. The foetus had to be removed. Somehow, Suzan never accepted that they had lost the child."

Dr. Gerrad signalled to his team, and they all moved out of the room that Suzan was in to give her space. Suzan called Ravi from her cellphone.

Ravi was on the deck of the ship, the wind whipping around him and the smell of salt filling the air. He looked out at the endless expanse of the ocean, his heart heavy with worry. His phone buzzed in his pocket, jolting him from his thoughts. He quickly answered, knowing it was the call he had been dreading.

"Hello, Suzan?" he said, his voice tight with anxiety.

"Ravi," Suzan's voice was faint and filled with despair. "They want to take the baby. They think... they think it's too dangerous to keep trying."

Ravi closed his eyes, his heart aching. "I know, love. I spoke to Dr. Gerrad. They're worried about you. The baby hasn't been responsive for days. They're scared for your life."

Suzan's voice cracked with emotion. "But Ravi, I want this child. I want to fight for it, no matter what. I can't just give up."

Ravi swallowed hard, trying to keep his voice steady. "Suzan, I want this child too. More than anything. But I can't lose you. The doctors say it's too dangerous. We have to trust them."

Tears streamed down Suzan's face as she clutched the phone. "Ravi, I've carried this baby for months. I've felt it move. I've dreamed of holding it in my arms. How can I just let it go?"

Ravi's own eyes filled with tears, his voice breaking.

"I know, Suzan. I know. But you're my 'everything'. You and the boys. We can't lose you. I can't lose you. Please, just listen to the doctors. Let them do what they think is best."

There was a long silence on the line, the only sound the distant crashing of waves against the ship. Finally, Suzan spoke, her voice barely above a whisper. "I'm so scared, Ravi. I'm scared of losing the baby. I'm scared of losing everything."

Ravi leaned against the railing, his heart heavy with pain. "I'm scared too, love. But we have to be strong. For each other, for the boys. We have to believe that we'll get through this. Together."

Suzan took a shaky breath, trying to gather her strength. "I don't know if I can do this without you here."

Ravi closed his eyes, wishing he could be there with her, hold her, reassure her. "You're the strongest person I know, Suzan. And you're not alone. I'm with you, even if I'm not there physically. I'm with you every step of the way. Trust the medical team."

As they spoke, Suzan was feeling better. Just then, Dr. Gerrad, Dr. Sunita, and his team entered the room again and came towards Suzan. "It's time," Dr. Sunita said softly.

Suzan's voice trembled. "They've come, Ravi. Love you, sailor."

As they ended the call, Ravi looked out at the ocean, his heart aching but filled with a renewed sense of determination. He would fight for their family, no matter what it took. And he knew that Suzan, with her incredible strength and courage, would do the same.

With the support and love of her husband and Shane and Shaun always cheering her up, Suzan was now ready to face her next challenge - Save her child.

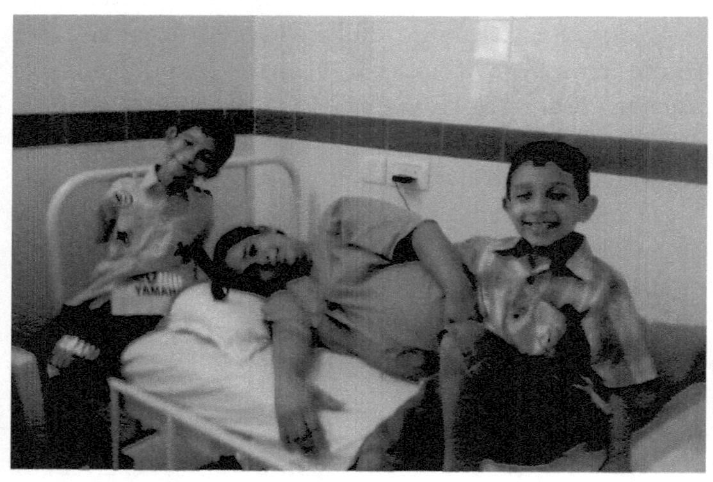

Suzan with Shane and Shaun

$$\triangleright\triangleright\triangleright$$

3

Do you believe in miracles, Dr. Gerrad?

—❦—

FERNANDES VILLA - TWO MONTHS EARLIER. Suzan, Ravi and their two boys Shane and Shaun lived in a quaint apartment in the bustling outskirts of Margao City, in Goa. They called their cosy home FERNANDES VILLA.

That particular afternoon, Suzan could not feel any movement of the child in her womb, so she immediately called for Dr. Gerrad, their family physician.

Dr. Gerrad is a distinguished paediatric cardiologist in his early fifties, known for his deep compassion and exceptional skills with children. Standing tall with a lean build, his grey-streaked hair and warm dark eyes give him a distinguished yet approachable appearance. His gentle smile and calm demeanour instantly put both patients and their families at ease.

A native of Goa, Dr. Gerrad has a particular fondness for Goan cuisine - Xacuti, Rechado and especially Bebinca. He often reminisces about his favourite dishes and even tries his hand at cooking them when time allows. His love for Goan food is well-known among his colleagues and friends, who often join him for a meal at a famous Goan restaurant.

In his earlier days, Dr. Gerrad was an avid basketball player. Though he no longer plays, he retains the discipline and teamwork spirit from his sports days, qualities that have significantly contributed to his professional success. He often shares stories from his basketball days with his young patients, using them to inspire and connect with them on a personal level.

Dr. Gerrad arrived within thirty minutes, accompanied by his assistant, Dr. Sunita who was a specialist in alternative medicine and technology. Suzan, as always, had her close friend Lisa with her. Gerrad sat with Suzan and Lisa at their residence. Suzan's face was etched with worry as she listened to the doctor.

Dr. Gerrad, looked at Suzan, understanding her fear. "During the last test at the hospital, there was a false alarm due to an issue with the Foetal-Doppler," he explained. "The device that monitors the baby's heartbeat was faulty, and there was a problem with the electrodes. They weren't picking up the signals correctly."

Lisa, visibly concerned, turned to Dr. Gerrad, her brow furrowed with worry. "What do you mean, problem with the electrodes?" she asked, her voice tinged with anxiety.

Lisa's eyes widened, and she exchanged a worried glance with Suzan. "So, there was nothing wrong with the baby?"

"Exactly," Dr. Gerrad confirmed. "It was a technical glitch. The position of the baby also made it difficult for the electrodes to get a clear reading"

Dr. Gerrad maintained a poker face, his tone honest but grave.

"But, it's still a rare case, Lisa." Dr. Gerrad then turned to Suzan, avoiding Lisa's suspicious glare at him, he continued, "Suzan, the system we used at the hospital was a bit, err... a bit... faulty. That's why we couldn't detect the heartbeat. But I also need to tell you that the baby's heart had stopped and started and is hardly detectable because the foetus is inverted." Suzan's eyes filled with tears. "This is the third time you've told me that we have lost our child and then you've miraculously found a heartbeat. Do you believe in miracles, Dr. Gerrad?"

"I believe in science and medicine. And medically, I still feel that this is going to be a difficult child," Dr. Gerrad replied carefully. "So I should give up and just let my child go back to the Lord? Difficult for you maybe, but the child will be fine. I know. A mother always knows," Suzan said defiantly. Dr. Gerrad sighed. "So? What do you want, a boy or a girl? You already have two wonderful boys." Dr. Gerrad tried to break the tension that was forming. He knew Suzan for a number of years and he himself wasn't very convinced if the foetus has survived. Suzan laughed weakly. "You know, Gerrad, after Shane and Shaun, we actually hope it's a girl. But Ravi and I decided long ago, that if it's a boy, his name will be with my initials S... and if it's a girl, it will be with his initials... R..."

Lisa turnedtowards Dr. Gerrad. Shane and Shaun who were playing outside in the yard, came barging into the room. They looked around and then sat by their pregnant mother's side. Suzan breathed deeply and cried a bit as she looked at Dr. Gerrad. "You've been saying that I have a 60-40 percent chance of survival. Hmmm! For this child, I'll take that chance. This child will be precious, Gerrad. And even though Ravi is sailing, I'm blessed to have my two pillars of strength right here with me." "Don't talk like that, 60-40 chance and all. I'm here for you as well. You know that..." Lisa added, trying to comfort her friend. "Yes, Lisa. You've always been there for us..." Suzan hugged Shane and Shaun close to her. "Lisa, click a photo of us, for memory's sake. Who knows? ..." Suzan said, trying to supress her fears with humour. Suzan felt that there was a possibility of her not surviving. "Shut up! I'll click one now because you all look cute, but that's the only reason..." Lisa replied, clicking a photo of Suzan. Shane and Shaun began to lighten the mood.

Shane placed his hands on his head like bull horns, making everyone laugh.

4

A Silent Echo

In the ICU, the atmosphere was tense and filled with the hum of medical equipment. Suzan lay on the hospital bed, surrounded by a flurry of doctors and nurses, her face pale and her body trembling with pain and fear. The sterile scent of antiseptic hung in the air, mingling with the muted sounds of urgent whispers and the rhythmic beeping of monitors. "Her blood pressure is dropping," one of the nurses announced, her voice tight with concern.

Dr. Gerrad, standing at the foot of Suzan's bed, barked orders to the team. "We need to stabilise her. Get the OR ready for an emergency C-section. We can't wait any longer."

AN HOUR LATER. Suzan's eyes darted around the room, wild with panic. Nurse Tina mumbles to another assistant Raju "Sad case. She's lost the child" Suzan hears her and reacts, "He's not gone. Don't say that!" "What's going on?" "Where is my Child?" "Do something...." Her voice was a mix of anger and desperation, each word cutting through the air like a knife.

Dr. Gerrad leaned closer to her, his expression grave but determined. "Suzan, listen to me. We're doing everything we can. You need to stay calm for the baby."

A nurse injected a sedative into Suzan's IV, and her thrashing gradually subsided, but her eyes still held a haunted look. "Please, save my baby," she whispered, her voice breaking.

On the other side, out on the galley of his ship, Ravi was pacing up and down by a port shore. His ship had docked. His phone began buzzing in his pocket. Ravi looked at the phone nervously. He paused, took a deep breath, and answered it. It was Dr. Gerrad calling from the hospital. "Hello, Ravi?" Dr. Gerrad inhaled deeply and composed himself. Suzan was looking around hurt and angrily. She yelled out. "Show me my child" "I can hear Suzan's voice. Gerrad? Why is she screaming? What happened? Gerrad..." Ravi's voice came through the phone, barely holding back tears.

Dr. Gerrad, his voice steady but strained, replied, "Ravi, we're facing complications. The foetus isn't responding, and Suzan's condition is critical. We're preparing for an emergency operation."

Ravi's heart sank. "Do whatever it takes, Gerrad. Just save them both."

As Dr. Gerrad hung up, he turned to his team. "We need to move now. Time is running out."

The medical staff worked with rapid precision, transferring Suzan to a gurney and wheeling her out of the ICU toward the operating room. The hallways blurred past in a frenzy of motion and noise. Suzan's grip on consciousness was fading, her mind drifting in and out of awareness.

In the operating room, the bright lights overhead shone harshly, casting stark shadows. The surgical team prepared swiftly, donning their gloves and masks. Dr. Sunita checked the monitors, ensuring everything was ready.

Dr. Gerrad took a deep breath and began the incision, his hands steady but his mind racing. The room was tense, the silence punctuated only by the soft beeps and whirs of the machines.

Outside, in the waiting area, Lisa paced back and forth. Shaun and Shane sitting at the side, nervously, in silence, their faces drawn with worry. Suzan's earlier screams still echoed in their minds, a haunting reminder of the stakes.

After what seemed like an eternity, the baby was finally delivered and had no heartbeat and no pulse. Dr. Gerrad bowed his head sadly and called Ravi again on his cellphone. He had to break the news to Ravi and in the background as Suzan was recovering from anaesthetic-sedation, Ravi answered the call.

"What's the verdict Doc? Is it a boy or a girl", Ravi asked very nervously.

"Ravi. I'm sorry. The baby was a boy. His echo was silent. He was still-born"

Dr. Gerrad said, his voice heavy with sorrow.

"I will not accept this. Give me my child. Ravi, help? Bloody liars. He's alive, Ravi!" Suzan's voice was aggressive yet weak.

"I'm sorry, Ravi," Dr. Gerrad repeated, cutting the call. He looked at Suzan with care and placed his hand on hers. "Stay strong for your boys, Suzan. Please..."

Suzan lay in the sterile hospital room, her heart shattered and her mind in turmoil. The silence of the room was deafening, a stark contrast to the joyful anticipation she had felt just days before as she entered her Seventh Month of pregnancy. The doctors had confirmed what she could not bring herself to accept: her child was gone, a stillborn angel she would never cradle in her arms. The pain was unlike anything she had ever known, a deep, soul-crushing agony that consumed her every thought. Tears streamed down her face as she clung to the hope that the doctors were wrong, that somehow her baby would awaken. She could not fathom a world without this child. Her heartache was compounded by a fierce, unyielding denial.

Ravi dropped down on his knees by the Port side, in despair. He looked up at the sky and made the Sign of the Cross. Back at the Hospital at the same time, Suzan had her hands folded in prayer too. She prayed with all her heart at the same moment too, both of them in unison across the boundaries.

"Sacred Heart of Jesus... I place my trust in You"

Their voices filled with hope and determination.

ᵱᵱᵱ

5

A Miracle?

Dr. Gerrad hurriedly approached Dr. Sunita and the supporting nurses who were still trying to revive the baby. A nurse, with a heavy heart, placed the lifeless infant in Suzan's arms. Suzan broke down, tears streaming down her face. The nurse began to lift the baby away when suddenly, the tiny fingers grasped Suzan's finger. Suzan's eyes widened in shock and hope as she pulled the baby back, holding him close to her heart. Dr. Sunita noticed the movement.

"*He held my hand, Doctor. He held my hand,*"

Suzan cried out.

Dr. Sunita, equally astonished, called out, "Dr. Gerrad, the baby responded!" Just as the room seemed to drown in a sea of despair, this sudden reflex from the child and Suzan's scream pierced through the silence. Dr. Gerrad's eyes widened in disbelief as he held the baby and felt its heartbeat flutter to life. "We've got a pulse! Get the crash cart, now!" he bellowed, his voice echoing in the silence of the OR. Nurses sprang into action. The once-sterile room now buzzed with a frenzied energy, every second stretching into an eternity. Suzan, her tear-streaked face turning towards the commotion, felt a glimmer of hope pierce through her sorrow. "Please, save my baby," she whispered. Dr. Gerrad's hands moved swiftly, his mind laser-focused on the delicate task of reviving the fragile heartbeat. The air was thick with anticipation, every breath held in suspense as they fought to pull the child from the brink of death. He had begun the resuscitation process, blowing breaths steadily into the baby's mouth and nose, repeating the actions in sequence. The ultrasound machine was reconnected, and a faint, uneven heartbeat flickered on the screen. Dr. Sunita sighed in relief and looked at Suzan.

"I shouldn't say this, but it's a miracle. He's alive."

Dr. Sunita ran out to deliver the news to Lisa, Shaun and Shane who were waiting anxiously for some update. Dr. Sunita told them everything that had happened in the OR.The baby, in the mean-time was quickly taken to an incubator. "Call Papa. Give him the good news, It's a boy!" Dr. Sunita said, her voice trembling with emotion. Shaun quickly dialled Ravi on his cellphone. "Hello...?" Ravi's voice was heavy with depression.

"Papa! It's a miracle. It's a boy. He's alive"

Shaun exclaimed, tears of joy streaming down his face.

"Praise God! Yes... Yes... Thank you, Jesus," Ravi replied, his voice filled with relief and gratitude.

A few days later, Shane, Shaun and Lisa were sitting by Suzan's side. Suzan was relieved. Shane was still curious and puzzled as well, as he kept looking at the baby in the incubator. "He's so small, Mumma. Let's call him Smallie," Shane said, his voice filled with awe. Suzan, though feeble, was relieved.

"The child was premature at 7 months and weighed just about 2.5 pounds."

ᗡᗡᗡ

Speaking to Suzan and Ravi about that particular day, here's what they had to say.

"I thought we had lost Shannon, and I was at risk too. But I think the baby was in a hurry to get out. He was very tiny and weak - one kilogram (2.5 Pounds) at birth, two months premature, but he had some sort of blessing, an inner strength. I think that strength comes from Ravi," Suzan said, her voice filled with admiration.

Ravi nods in agreement. "Yes, he's strong, but not like me. He's strong, just like his mother. I was busy sailing and preparing for the future. She managed a lot of things on her own with very little help. At that time, I knew everything that was going on, but I was helpless. Even though I was at sea, I felt like a fish out of water on that particular day".

Ravi and Suzan held hands as they poured out their journey to me.

ᗡᗡᗡ

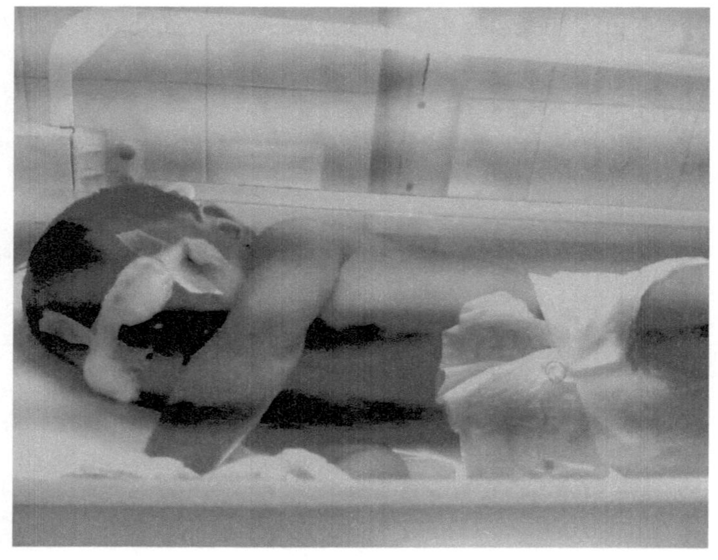

A first look in the incubator

6

Hello Shanon!

Suzan lay on the hospital bed, her heart heavy with the uncertainty of her just born child. They named him Shanon. A name starting with the alphabet 'S', as they had earlier decided. A name with Suzan's initials. Shanon had been declared stillborn during her pregnancy, only to miraculously survive. The doctors were baffled, calling it a rare and extraordinary case. But to Suzan and her family, it was nothing short of a miracle. Shanon's heart was extremely faint, and his vision was slightly impaired, but Suzan never lost hope. With the steadfast support of her sons, Shane and Shaun, she fought on, determined to bring her child into the world. Suzan's resilience was a beacon of strength for her family, guiding them through the darkest times.

Ravi, working tirelessly to make ends meet, found it hard to be away from his family during these trying times. His job kept him at sea for long periods, leaving Suzan to navigate the challenges at home. He would often argue with Suzan over the phone about Shanon's condition, trying to offer comfort despite the physical distance between them.

"There's nothing wrong with him," Ravi would insist, his voice crackling through the phone. "Don't stress, Suzan. Stop panicking." But Suzan knew the truth. She felt the fragility of Shanon's life with every beat of her own heart. Yet, she distributed her time, love, and affection equally among her three children, never making any distinctions. She believed in treating them all with the same care and devotion, despite Shanon's unique challenges.

Ravi's reassurances were often all he could offer during stormy weather, rain, or shine. Deep down, he knew he had to stay strong to keep Suzan strong until he could return home. The weight of responsibility on his shoulders was immense, but he bore it with a sense of duty and love for his family. Shanon was in a special incubator. Each doctor had their own treatment recommendations and the tension in the Fernandes household grew. Suzan's faith in Shanon's survival never faltered, but she couldn't ignore the fears that crept into her mind. She prayed fervently, hoping for a miracle that would allow her child to thrive despite the odds.

The day Shanon was born was a day of both joy and fear. Suzan's labour through a C-section operation, was long and arduous, and the medical team was on high alert. Ravi, unable to be there in person, paced the deck of his ship, his heart pounding with anxiety. He knew Suzan needed him, but all he could do was pray and wait for news. He recalled the drama during the birth of Shanon, being declared stillborn - dead and then the miracle of him coming to life. Both Ravi and Suzan felt, at that moment, an overwhelming surge of love and relief. He was small and fragile, but he was alive. His tiny heart beat faintly, a testament to his resilience and the power of a mother's love.

Deep down in her heart, Suzan instinctively knew there was something special about Shanon and she vowed to cherish every moment with him. The journey ahead would be challenging, but she was ready to face it with the same determination that had brought her this far.

Shanon's survival was a beacon of hope, a reminder that miracles were possible even in the darkest circumstances. They both knew the road ahead would be tough, especially Ravi and he was now even more determined to offer more support to his family every step of the way.

As the days turned into weeks and weeks into months, Shanon's health remained delicate. Suzan and Ravi continued to argue about his condition, but their love for their son never diminished. They both knew that Shanon's journey was just beginning, and they were prepared to face whatever challenges lay ahead, with Shane and Shaun by their side. Suzan's fight to bring Shanon into the world had taught them all to be resilient, and that strength would carry them through the trials to come. Shanon's presence in their lives was a constant reminder of the power of love and faith. His journey was a testament to the resilience of the human spirit and the unbreakable bond of family. And later, as Suzan held her son close, she knew that together, they could overcome any obstacle and embrace the miracles that life had in store for them.---

ᗏᗏᗏ

7
Skating Dreams and Fading Lights

KINGS SCHOOL, 14-MAY-2012. Five years later. The school bell rang, and a group of children, including five-year-old Shanon, exited the building. Suzan was waiting at the entrance for Shanon. He spotted his mother and ran towards her. Suddenly, he clutched his chest, his heart racing. Suzan held him as he collapsed, blacking out. She began opening his shirt and rubbing his chest. In the darkness of the blackout, Shanon could hear sounds of an ambulance siren and noises as paramedics from the School rushed in and he recalls hearing a constant beeping sound as he passed out at school. Shanon was immediately transferred to the hospital where he was born. ~~

Life is like a free-flowing river, and like a river, Shanon's life too was not defined... He questioned his purpose, his very existence. It was here that his journey began. In this very hospital, where he was born - dead.

"And yet by some miracle, I am alive. Shanon says this with a strong determination in his voice, as he

recalls that day. I was around 5 years old at that time. Later I was home studying and I could see mumma's worried look on her face all the time, but I always tried to make her smile. Though I was named Shanon, my family nicknamed me 'Smallie'. Because I was tiny when I was born, and I love being called by that name, but only by my family."

Shanon was sitting on the school bench, watching all the children play. They were running about, laughing, and skating. A few older boys passed by on skates.

"Hey, Fatso! Wanna bounce around on the playground?" one of them jeered.

Other boys and girls nearby laughed behind Shanon's back. He got up to walk away.

"Earthquake!" shouted one of the boys.

Just as Shanon smiled weakly and began to walk away, a huge thud and lots of murmuring sounds distracted him. Both the bullies were flattened on the floor.

A girl's voice screamed, "Not so fat and dangerous now, are you?"

"Help!" shouted the other boy.

"Leave Shanon alone, you bullies," said a familiar friend's voice. The bullies ran away with everyone around laughing. Shanon smiled, his face lighting up and beaming with pride.

"Thanks, Emily. And to you as well, Paul," Shanon said.

Emily and Paul had been friends with Shanon since the day he first joined school. Emily was small and looked fragile but was tenacious and aggressive when it came to protecting Shanon. Paul was tall, well-built, and huge for his age. He hated bullies and was always looking out for Shanon.

They sat at the play area watching the other children skate by.

"Why are you so quiet now? They've left and won't trouble you again," said Emily.

"They won't dare bully anyone when I'm around, so cheer up, Shanon," Paul added.

"It's not that," said Shanon mildly.

"Then what is it?" asked Emily.

Shanon stood up determined, "I want to skate," he said. "I know about my condition and all, but I really wanna skate."

The school bell rang, signalling the end of the break, and they all walked towards their classrooms.

"I'm sure you will skate someday, Shanon," said Emily soothingly.

ᐅᐅᐅ

Dr. Gerrad wasn't too convinced of this idea, but he knew Suzan wasn't one to give in. The school said they were not yet fully equipped with a proper skating rink. Suzan, who was brought up in a very controlled environment growing up, had no clue as to how to travel or be independent. Ravi was the one who usually handled everything, but things were changing after the birth of Shanon. The place suggested for skating was far away from her city in a nearby state that had a skating rink with all the facilities.

ᐅᐅᐅ

There were many debates on Suzan pushing limits with Shanon. Shanon always wanted to be active and would look around at children in his school playing, skating, and running. He knew that if he tried, he could be in big trouble, but skating was something that was building up a deep sense of wanting in him. He approached his parents but was initially told by his dad that skates were very expensive and that currently they could not afford them.

ﭛﭛﭛ

"Shanon says he will be careful, Ravi. King's School has put me in touch with a special instructor in Belagavi (formerly Belgaum) and they're willing to guide him" said Suzan defiantly.

"And if he falls? Or gets injured in his current condition?" Ravi retorted.

"Then let him fall, like any normal child would. We will address that issue at that time. Please think about it," Suzan responded.

"Are the skates really very expensive? Or are you just saying that to put me off from going ahead?" asked Suzan.

"You're anyway going to do what you feel is best, I know that. And no, the skates are not expensive, it's just that I worry," Ravi said with a sigh.

Ravi's worry was understandable, but Suzan's determination was unshakeable. She saw the spark in Shanon's eyes whenever he talked about skating, and she knew that denying him this dream would be crushing. They had already overcome so much as a family; she believed they could handle this challenge too.

The following week, Suzan took Shanon to Belagavi in a Public Bus to meet the Skating instructor. The rink was bustling with kids of all ages, gliding effortlessly on the smooth surface. Shanon's eyes widened with excitement as he took in the scene. The instructor, a kind man named John, greeted them warmly and assured Suzan that they would take all necessary precautions.

Shanon's first few attempts were wobbly, but John was patient and encouraging. Shane and Shaun had come along for support (Suzan always carted them with her, anywhere she went), cheering Shanon on from the side-lines. Every time he stumbled, they would shout words of encouragement, lifting his spirits.

"You're doing great, Smallie!" Shane called out.

"Keep your balance!" Shaun added.

Shanon's progress was slow but steady. Each session, he improved a little more, and his confidence grew. Suzan watched with pride as her son persevered, his determination shining through. She knew there would be challenges ahead, but seeing Shanon's joy made every effort worthwhile.

Back in school, Shanon's break time was filled with his skating and driving adventures to Belagavi and back. Paul, Emily and a few other children, gathered around him. Shanon was making friends as the days passed.

Ravi, still anxious, found himself calling more frequently, asking about Shanon's progress. Hearing about Shanon's determination and the support from the School and Shanon's friends, Emily and Paul reassured him, a little bit. He was learning to trust Suzan's judgement and Shanon's resilience.

Weeks turned into months, and Shanon became more proficient on his skates.

Says Suzan,

"I would travel by bus at first on holidays, or weekends and later on I learnt to drive our car. We rushed at any opportunity to go to Belagavi to skate and progress was showing. He did have one or two bad falls suddenly, but that was nothing that I was overly worried about at that time. I did consult Dr. Gerrad and Dr. Jason as well and they advised

taking Shanon to Bangalore for treatment. He may need a pacemaker or a surgical solution."

"**Authors Note:** *As I continued chatting with Ravi when writing this chapter, he recalls that even the most seasoned doctors were baffled and puzzled with this rear condition. Shanon was the boy that was not supposed to have made it and suddenly, now we're getting him ready for the Olympics. Of Course I was being a bit sarcastic, but I was worried within as well. Somehow, a part of me refused to accept that anything was wrong with Smallie, and on the flip side, Suzan's risks were bothering me when I was away.*"

Though Shanon's blackouts were getting more frequent, He had by now even started participating in small skating events at the rink and in school. His health remained a concern, but with careful monitoring and the right precautions, he managed to stay safe.

ᐅᐅᐅ

8
The School Games

The day had dawned for the school games, and Shanon was set to participate against some of the best skaters in the school. Suzan, Shane, and Shaun were there, eagerly cheering him on. Emily, Paul, and all his classmates shouted, "Shanon, Shanon!" After a long journey, the moment had finally come. Shanon took his position at the starting line, nerves and excitement coursing through him. As the whistle blew, he took off with the other skaters, all whizzing around the makeshift school rink. Shanon started slow, conserving his energy, but as the race progressed, he picked up pace. After a third of the race had been completed, he saw an opportunity and managed to overtake several skaters, moving into second position. The crowd's cheers grew louder, urging him on.

As they neared the final leg of the race, Shanon was toe-to-toe with the leader. The finish line was in sight, just one last corner before the straight stretch to the end. Taking a calculated risk, Shanon took a wide berth and swung in just before the corner, overtaking the leader and moving into first position. Now in the innermost lane and leading the race, Shanon felt a sudden numbness grip his body. The lights around him turned to a glow, and everything slowly hazed out. Just as he rounded the final corner, his body gave way. He was neck to neck with the school champion, he felt his body surge as he attempted to cross the finish line. He collapsed in a heap and slid across the rink at full speed. His helmet fell off, and he came to a halt mere inches from hitting the side wall.

As everything began to fade from Shanon's eyes, he could hear the distant, frantic screams of his mother, Suzan. Suzan rushed to Shanon's side, his bothers and friends close behind. Suzan's heart pounded as she swiftly opened Shanon's shirt and expertly recalled all that the doctors had taught her on CPR. King's School had a dedicated Medical Wing and in a matter of moments, the medics from the school rushed in and continued to assist as Suzan administered CPR.

"Cardiopulmonary resuscitation (CPR) combines rescue breathing (mouth-to-mouth) and chest compressions to temporarily pump enough blood to the brain until specialised treatment is available."

Shane and Shaun supported their mother and watched the medics work, their faces pale with concern. Emily and Paul, usually so strong, were on the verge of tears, helplessly watching their friend. "Please, please be okay," Suzan whispered, her eyes never leaving Shanon. After what felt like an eternity, one of the medics looked up and nodded. "He's breathing. We need to get him to the hospital immediately."

Suzan let out a breath she didn't realise she had been holding. "Thank you," she whispered, following the medics as they carefully lifted Shanon onto a stretcher.

At the hospital, the doctors ran a series of tests to determine what had caused Shanon's collapse. Ravi, who had been at sea, was contacted immediately. He was given special leave and dropped everything, rushing immediately for home. After two long flights, rough weather and a long road trip, he finally made his way back as quickly as he could, his heart heavy with worry for his son.

As Ravi reached, hours passed in agonising suspense before the doctors finally emerged with answers. Dr. Gerrad, his face etched with concern, spoke with urgency. "Shanon experienced a severe episode of fatigue, worsened by his heart condition," he explained. "His heart rate plummeted unexpectedly, and we had to administer emergency medication to stabilise him."

Suzan's heart raced. "Is he going to be alright?" Dr. Gerrad nodded cautiously. "We managed to bring his heart rate back to normal, but it was a close call. His condition is more volatile than we anticipated. We've ordered an immediate round of intensive monitoring and additional tests to ensure there are no hidden complications." Ravi asked "What kind of complications?" Dr. Gerrad sighed. "There could be several issues at play, from arrhythmias to potential blockages. We need to keep a close eye on him for the next 24 hours. Any further episodes could be dangerous." "But he's going to be okay, right?" Ravi asked, his voice breaking a bit. The doctor nodded. "With rest and proper care, he should recover. However, he will need to be monitored closely, and we'll need to reassess his activities to ensure something like this doesn't happen again."

Relief washed over Suzan and Ravi. "Thank you," Suzan said, tears streaming down her face.

As Shanon slowly regained consciousness, he found himself surrounded by his family and friends. Suzan held his hand, her eyes filled with love and relief. "Mom?" Shanon croaked, his voice weak. "I'm here, sweetheart," Suzan said softly. "You're going to be okay." Shanon managed a small smile. "Did I... did I win?"

Suzan chuckled through her tears. "You were winning, my brave boy and came in second, with a Silver Medal, just before you collapsed." Shanon sulked. Emily and Paul stepped forward, their faces filled with concern and admiration. "You were amazing out there, Shanon," Paul said. "We're so proud of you." Shaun beams and puts the medal around Shanon's neck. Everyone applauds. Emily nodded. "Just promise us you'll be more careful next time, okay?"

Shanon nodded, his eyes heavy with exhaustion and looked at everyone around him. "I promise" he replied.

ppp

Shanon with one of his many skating medals!

9
Shanon's Battle

Shanon sat on his bed, surrounded by a stack of books and a few scattered electronic toys. Suzan hovered nearby, her worried eyes fixed on him. "Smallie, it's time for your medication," she said, her voice gentle but firm. Shanon reluctantly nodded and reached for the pill bottle on his bedside table, struggling to open it with his trembling hands. Suzan gently took the bottle and opened it for him, her heart aching at the sight of her son's struggle. Suddenly, the phone in Shanon's bedroom rang, breaking the heavy silence. Suzan rushed to answer it, hoping for good news. "Hello? Jason? Oh! Okay, Doctor. No, I understand. Yes, I will inform Ravi when he calls," she said, her voice tinged with sadness.

The voice on the other end had delivered bad news, causing Suzan's shoulders to slump in defeat. She hung up the phone, trying to hold back tears. She touched her forehead to Shanon's and held him. "That was Dr. Jason's office. They're postponing your surgery again. They're not sure about your condition, so they want me to speak with Dr. Gerrad and then with Dr. Carol Walters from the US. She will call here in some time. Your cousin Dr. Jesuina from Australia has briefed them," Suzan explained, her voice soft but steady.

Shanon's face fell, disappointment written all over his features. But Suzan refused to let despair take over. "It's okay, son. We'll figure something out. Things always work out in the end. I have faith, and you know Dr. Jesuina is investigating your case too," Suzan said, her voice filled with determination.

"Okay, Mom! You are my Superwoman and Wonder Woman too. You're my hero," Shanon said, bursting into a smile. Just then, the landline phone extension in the room rang. Suzan answered it. "Hello!"

"Hello, is that Suzan?" a voice asked. "Yes. Doctor... Walters?" "Yes, Carol Walters. You can call me Carol," the doctor replied. "Yes, Doctor Carol," Suzan said.

"I've studied Shanon's case papers and his prognosis as well. I also had a long talk with Dr. Jesuina to discuss Shanon's condition," Dr. Walters explained.

"Okay, Doctor... And?"

"What Shanon has is extremely rare, from birth asphyxia through various bouts of T-Loc, somnambulism. It could be Kleine–Levin syndrome, also called 'Sleeping Beauty syndrome.' Sorry, I mean I'm reading the reports from a doctor's point of view," Dr. Walters continued.

> **"Kleine-Levin syndrome is an extremely rare disorder characterised by the need for excessive amounts of sleep (hyper-somnolence), excessive eating (compulsive hyperphagia), and behavioural abnormalities."**

"Carry on, Doctor. I've read up on these ailments and studied his reports. I do value your time and consult," Suzan said. "He also has syncope and paroxysmal atrial tachycardia," Dr. Walters added, pausing for a moment. "Ah, of course, you've read the reports, dear. So, moving on, I've also spoken to Dr. Raghvendra from the Bangalore Hospital, and he mentioned issues that can be resolved by them." "Yes, Doctor. Shanon faints suddenly in between any activity. Children make fun of him," Suzan said. Shanon looked over, watching his mother talk on the phone. "Mom! Tell her the other kids were sometimes mean to me. Not Emily and Paul, but most of the others, and after I won the silver medal, everything changed."

Suzan smiled at Shanon. "Shanon says to say that some children were mean to him and now everyone's attitude has changed after he won a medal. Anyway, what do you suggest, Doctor Carol?" "Tell Shanon he's a 'One in a million' kid. He's special and that he will fight back and smile through this one day," Dr. Walters replied. "Yes, Doctor Carol," Suzan replied.

"Suzan, Dr. Raghvendra is right. Do the procedure, and they will insert a device called a loop recorder or ICM. You have someone there who can explain it all to you, right?" Dr. Walters asked.

"Loop recorder. Yes, they had mentioned that to me as well. Dr. Sunita will be coming over with my friend Lisa in some time. She's Dr. Gerrad's assistant," Suzan explained.

"Fantastic. If there's anything you need, I'm just a call away," Dr. Walters said.

"Thank you, Doctor Carol. I'm feeling much better after talking to you," Suzan said, her voice filled with gratitude.

"I'll keep in touch, Suzan. You take care. Tell Shanon that he will be fine," Dr. Walters said before disconnecting the call.

Suzan began walking towards Shanon. Just then, the doorbell rang. Suzan opened the door to find Lisa and Dr. Sunita standing there with sympathetic looks on their faces. "Hey, Suzan. How's everything going?" Lisa asked.

Suzan forced a smile, trying to hide her exhaustion. "Oh, you know, just the usual challenges."

"Did that doctor from America call you? That's what we're here to discuss, dear," Dr. Sunita said.

"Yes, she called."

"...and?" Lisa prompted.

"She said that I will have to get an ICM inserted surgically into Shanon," Suzan explained.

"What's an ICM?" Lisa asked.

"It's an Insertable Cardiac Monitor. A transmitter that wirelessly collects heart data and makes it available to us for monitoring. It will be implanted in his chest, surgically," Dr. Sunita explained.

"But is it safe? What are the side effects?" Suzan asked.

"Shanon has had several symptoms, dear. Severe dizziness, syncope, somnambulism, and episodes of paroxysmal atrial tachycardia. It means his heart has short, fast beats. You know he needs the surgery, dear," Dr. Sunita said, her voice filled with concern.

"He'll be okay, Suzan. Shanon will be fine," Lisa added, giving her friend a comforting hug.

Suzan nodded, her heart heavy with worry but filled with hope.

ᗊᗊᗊ

10

I have the Power!

Suzan recalls that Shanon was extremely sensitive to any medication. He would break out or react and often experienced side effects from very simple treatments. He was prepped twice for a pacemaker, but both times the procedures were cancelled. After extensive global consultations, it was finally decided to go ahead with the installation of an Insertable Cardiac Monitor (ICM) in his chest. Shanon was probably one of the youngest children in the world to undergo this procedure, and the 'Loop Recorder' was quite expensive.

First, they tried a **Holter Monitor** to externally track his condition as it was non-intrusive. They got it attached and returned to Goa. However, one of the monitors fell off while he was playing on a weekend at the Mall. Suzan was immediately called from Bangalore, asking why it had stopped. The next day, she left for Bangalore where they replaced it with another Holter in the same place.

A few days later, Shanon got an infection, and the Second Holter was removed. The expenses were mounting with these experiments and trials.

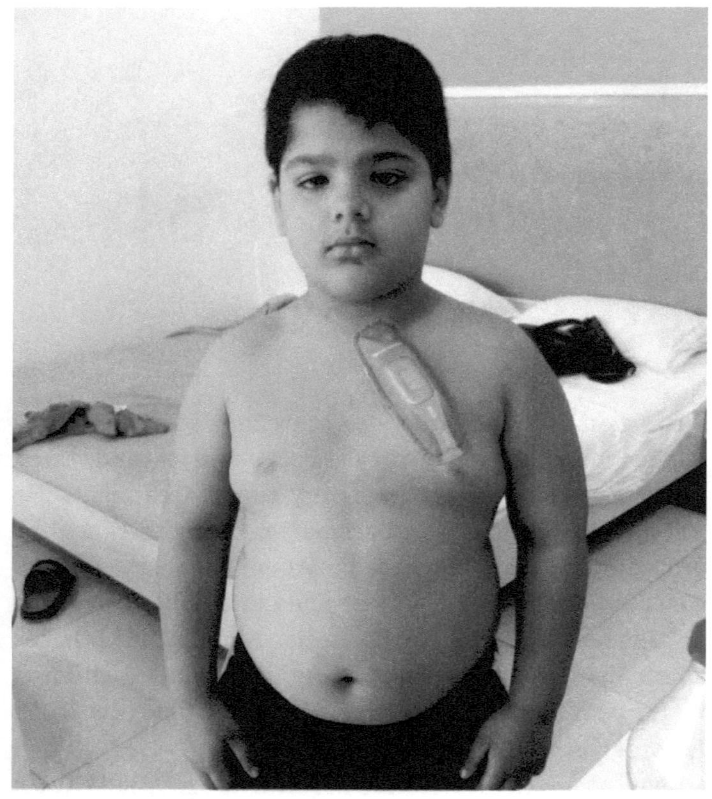

Shanon with his Holter....

Once the infection was cleared and totally healed, the doctor told Suzan about the loop recorder again. She wasn't ready for it. She spoke to Dr. Jason and Dr. Gerrad, who both insisted that they must proceed.

Shanon had the ICM (Loop Recorder) installed in his chest. Although Shanon's heart seizures and collapses did not stop, the ICM immediately sent signals to the receiver, allowing Suzan to monitor his condition. This data collection was a major step in the hunt for a solution, a cure, anything.

Suzan always treated all her boys equally, husband sometimes included. Shanon later stated that he felt he had superpowers—like Iron Man—with the device in his chest. "I have the power," he would often say, and then Shane and Shaun would playfully rough him up.

The Loop Recorder was inserted in Shanon for five years. He did have an issue once, as the battery wore off and it had to be replaced. Expenses were building up, and loans against their gold and working overtime helped them survive those difficult five years.

Through it all, Suzan remained hopeful, always believing that a cure or a better treatment was just around the corner. But as the years passed, the uncertainty of Shanon's condition loomed large. They had come a long way, but the road ahead was still unclear.

Would the ICM continue to help? Would they finally find a lasting solution? Suzan's thoughts were filled with questions, but one thing remained certain: they would face whatever came their way together, with unwavering determination and love.

ppp

11

Five Years of Waiting

Five years had passed since Shanon had the Insertable Cardiac Monitor (ICM) installed in his chest. In that time, he had grown from a delicate five-year-old to a vibrant ten-year-old, navigating life with courage and resilience. The journey had been filled with challenges, but also moments of joy and achievement. Shanon's grades in school improved steadily. He found a new passion in acting and was cast in a short film titled **Mumma! I Got Your Cigarettes** and the following year in a film – **ONE PUFF!** His performance was well-received, showcasing his budding talent. This accomplishment was a source of immense pride for Suzan and Ravi, who had always encouraged their children to pursue their interests despite the obstacles.

Ravi was home for Christmas, a rare but cherished occasion. Shaun and Shane were excelling in their academics. Shane, with his entrepreneurial spirit, opened a catering firm called The Goan Charcutier, creating and selling various gourmet products. Shaun, on the other hand, was exploring his talents and had taken on a role guiding and mentoring students, helping them unlock their potential. Despite the successes and happy moments, uncertainty still loomed over the Fernandes family. Shanon's ICM had to be replaced twice during the five years, and each time, the cost was exorbitant. This Christmas, however, was special. For once, they had a wonderful celebration, filled with laughter and warmth.

The coming new year, saw Ravi back out at sea, working tirelessly to provide for his family, enduring the rough seas and long periods away from home. He had promised to be back for Shanon's 10th Birthday. Time began to flow as fast as the water that flowed under the vessels that Ravi sailed on.

16th August 2017, the day had finally dawned. As Family and friends gathered to celebrate Shanon's 10th birthday. There was a mix of joy and apprehension in the air. The family had come a long way, but they knew the time had come to remove the ICM. The future was once again uncertain, and the looming question of what lay ahead weighed heavily on their minds. Shanon could sense the tension. "Mumma, Papa, it's going to be okay," he said, his voice steady despite his young age. "I feel strong, like Iron Man." Suzan and Ravi exchanged a glance, both feeling a mixture of pride and worry. Shanon had always shown a remarkable ability to stay positive and strong, even in the face of his health challenges.

"Yes, Shanon. You are strong," Suzan replied, her voice filled with determination. "We'll face whatever comes next, together."

The day of the ICM removal surgery approached quickly. Dr. Jason and Dr. Gerrad were there to guide them, and the whole family rallied around Shanon, offering their support and encouragement. As Shanon was prepped for the procedure, he looked at his family and smiled. "I have the power," he said, echoing his favourite mantra.

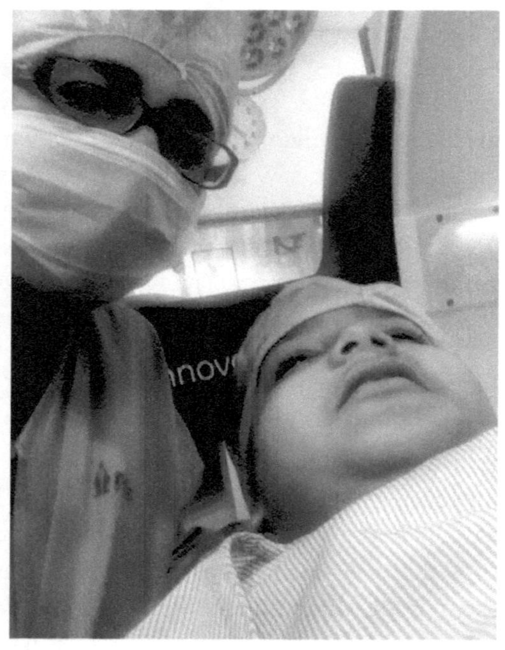

Suzan with Shanon for the removal of the ICM

ᗡᗡᗡ

12
Uncertainty!

After the removal of his ICM, Shanon's future was a question mark, a canvas of unknowns and uncertainties. The successful surgery had brought a sense of relief, but it was tempered by the knowledge that Shanon's battle was far from over. Shanon lay in his hospital bed, his chest bandaged, feeling a mix of exhaustion and hope. The device that had been his lifeline for the past five years was gone, and while he felt lighter, he also felt vulnerable. His body, still sensitive to medications, reacted unpredictably to treatments, and each day was a new challenge.

Suzan sat by his side, holding his hand, her face a blend of relief and worry. Ravi was beside her, his thoughts heavy with the uncertain future. Shane, Shaun, and Lisa were a constant presence, their support unwavering. Shane was prepping to get his first job on a Tourist Cruise Ship abroad. A perfect blend of his father's profession and his desire to travel the world as well. Shaun was pursuing academics, music and sound design and is looking to a creative future in the film and music industry.

Despite their busy lives, their priority remained their brother, their family.

"Mumma, what happens now?" Shanon asked, his voice soft but steady.

Suzan squeezed his hand gently. "Now, we take it one day at a time, Smallie. We face each challenge as it comes and we keep fighting."

The days following the surgery were filled with a whirlwind of medical appointments and new medications. Shanon's reactions varied, some days better than others. There were moments when the shadow of near-death incidents loomed close, but each time, Shanon fought back with a resilience that amazed everyone around him. Ravi, when not at sea, spent every moment he could with the family. The rough seas seemed like a distant memory compared to the storms they faced with Shanon's health. Yet, he remained the pillar of strength for Suzan and the boys.

One evening, as they all gathered in the living room, Shanon looked around at his family. The uncertainty of his condition still lingered, but the love and support of his family gave him strength. "Hey, Mumma, do you remember the day we found out about the ICM?" Shanon asked suddenly. Suzan smiled, her eyes misty with memories. "I do, Smallie. It was a tough decision, but it gave us five years of data and time to understand your condition better." Shanon nodded. "And now, without it, I'm free but I feel like maybe my powers are taken away after it was removed." Ravi walked over and placed a hand on Shanon's shoulder. "You've always been a fighter, son. And we're all here, fighting with you, what's your power? The love of our family and our faith." Shanon beams with happiness from that answer.

The family continued to face each day with a mixture of hope and fear, but they were united in their determination to give Shanon the best life possible. They celebrated the small victories, like a day without a reaction or a good report from the doctor. They cherished each moment, knowing that uncertainty was a part of their journey but not the definition of it.

As the months passed, Shanon continued to live his life, attending school, participating in activities, and spending time with his friends Emily and Paul. He embraced each day with a bravery that inspired everyone around him.

On Shanon's eleventh birthday, the family gathered to celebrate. The house was filled with laughter and joy, a stark contrast to the dark atmosphere that had often prevailed earlier.

Shanon blew out the candles on his cake, a wide smile on his face. "Here's to another year of fighting and living," he said, raising his slice of cake. "To fighting and living," the family echoed, their voices filled with love and hope.

A Short film on the life of Shanon, titled "A SILENT ECHO!" was completed in July 2024. The film story was written by the Author of this book - Jojo D'Souza with inputs from Ravi and Suzan Fernandes. The project was supported technically by Big Banner Entertainment and Media LLP (Deepak and Chandan Bandekar) and was directed by Ankita D'Souza (also the Art Director of the project). The Executive Producer Rajkumari D'Souza (Admin and Post Production Head at Big Banner) and Jojo D'Souza (Creative Head at Big Banner) and their entire team worked tirelessly to ensure the completion of this film, staying as true as possible to the original story of Shanon. This Book is a tribute to the belief of one family that is best summed up in the closing that follows -

10th **July, 2024.** Suzan sat at the dining table, writing in her journal. Shannon's voice could be heard in the background, excitedly telling Shane about his day. Suzan paused, listening to her son's laughter, her heart swelling with love. Shane had just called from a Port near the United Kingdom, mentioning that they were about to dock and he had a hearty conversation with Shanon, Shaun and Suzan. Ravi joined in as well.

Suzan looks at her journal. She wrote, **"Life has tested us in ways we never imagined, but through it all, we've found strength in our love for each other. Shanon's journey has just begun, and I know he will continue to inspire us with his courage and determination. Our miracle boy, our warrior, our heart."**

Suzan closed the journal, looking up at Ravi, who smiled at her from across the room. They both knew that no matter what challenges lay ahead, they would face them together, with love, faith, and an unbreakable bond. In the distance from their balcony they could see the sun setting calmly.

Ravi and the family gathered together and folded their hands in Prayer, giving thanks to the Lord for the Gift of Mumma Suzan and Shanon and their family. Everyone chorused "Amen". As they watched the sun setting, Ravi looked at his family and said

"There's always hope at the end of the horizon!"

♥♥♥

Epilogue

The years that followed are a testament to Shanon's resilience and the unwavering support of his family. The path was paved with challenges and moments of fear, but also with incredible strength and love. Shanon's condition still remains a constant battle, but he faces it with courage and determination. The uncertainty of Shanon's future is always present, but it is met with a fierce resolve to live each day to the fullest. The medical advancements and the continuous care from doctors worldwide have played a crucial role in managing his health, but it is the love and support from his family that truly made the difference. In the end, it is the journey, filled with love, support, and the unyielding spirit of family, that has defined their lives. Shanon's story is one of courage, resilience, and the power of love to overcome even the greatest uncertainties.

᭡᭡᭡

Shanon has just completed his Grade 10 (Class 10) with constant support from the family and especially the Management, Principal, Teachers and Staff including the Medical team at The Kings School, Goa. He passed with a Distinction and is now pursuing further studies.

Shanon sums up by saying

> "*I want to explore River and Sea Tourism, Boat / Crocodile and Bird Cruises like my Papa did when he was young. I also want to explore acting, I love photography and creating comic concepts as well. I am in a happy space because my Mumma and Papa as well as my brothers Shane and Shaun, and my*

Papa's friend, the author of this book - (Uncle) Jojo all took time to take care of me, hear my story and motivate me to live my dreams.."

The Fernandes Family a few years ago...

ᐅᐅᐅ

Shaun And Shane

As this book concludes, Shaun is exploring a career in film, sound and entertainment. Having being a mentor / teacher at Don Bosco Schools at various places, he was awarded for some of his writing works and was a very loved and respected teacher to a number of students.

His passion has always been Creative works, including designing artworks as well. He learnt music and plays the violin and the trumpet too.

(L-R) Shaun & Shane

ppp

Shane is out at sea, following in his father's footsteps. He is on board a cruise vessel in the catering department, travelling and exploring the world and its cuisine.

His company the GOAN CHACUTIER is still budding in Goa and he plans to grow in the food industry.

Brothers for life!

ppp

A Tribute From Shaun!

As I stand at the crossroads of my journey, exploring a career in film, sound, and entertainment, I find myself reflecting on the incredible path that has led me here. From my time as a mentor and teacher at various Don Bosco Schools, to being awarded for my writing and gaining the respect and love of my students, my passion for creativity has always been a guiding force in my life. But none of this would have been possible without the unwavering support and love of my parents, Suzan and Ravi.

Mum, your strength and resilience are the bedrock of our family. Watching you navigate the challenges and triumphs of raising Shanon, while always ensuring that Shane and I never felt neglected, has been nothing short of inspiring. Your ability to find joy in the smallest moments and to turn adversity into an opportunity for growth has taught me the true meaning of love and sacrifice.

"You have been our guiding light, our rock, and our endless source of comfort."

Your dedication to our family, even in the face of the toughest times, is a testament to your boundless love and courage.

Dad, your determination and hard work have shown me the value of perseverance.

"As a chef and seaman, you faced the rough seas and stormy oceans to provide for us, always putting our needs above your own."

Your passion for cooking and your commitment to our family have been constant reminders of the strength of your character. Even when you were miles away, we felt your presence, your love, and your unwavering support. You taught us that life is not always easy, but with determination and a strong will, we can overcome any obstacle.

Growing up, you both encouraged my creative pursuits, from designing artworks to learning music. Whether it was playing the violin and trumpet or diving into the world of rock and metal music, you always supported my passions. This foundation of love and encouragement has allowed me to explore my talents and carve out a path in the creative world.

As I venture into film and entertainment, I carry with me the lessons you both have taught me. Mum, your strength and compassion are the pillars upon which I build my dreams. Dad, your hard work and dedication are the driving forces that push me to achieve my goals. You have both shown me that with love, perseverance, and a bit of creativity, anything is possible.

"Thank you for being my role models, my supporters, and my biggest cheerleaders."

This journey is as much yours as it is mine, and I am forever grateful for the love and sacrifices you have made to help me become who I am today.

ϷϷϷ

When 'Smallie' was to be born, Shaun and I were so excited. From the time we knew Mum was expecting, we were filled with joy. We were kids back then, around 6 or 7 years old, but we wanted to help around. We would assist Mum in any little way we could, like watering the plants and helping around the house.

Then, soon the day came when Mum was suddenly rushed to the hospital because the baby had to be taken out. I remember being scared, excited, and nervous all at once, but by the grace of God, things went smoothly, and we got to meet our baby brother for the first time. Even after he was brought home, like I said, there wasn't much help around since Dad also wasn't here, so it was up to Shaun and me to take care of our little brother. Nobody forced us or anything; rather, we wanted to help.

We loved him and still do so much. I always say, and I've told him as well,

"To us, you are not our brother but you are like our own son because we have taken care of you like that."

Then as time went by, we realised that he is not like the other kids, very different in many ways. So Mum started her investigations, which took us all the way to Bangalore. There, we found out all of his problems. From that point, it was a constant struggle, but we managed. Sometimes there wasn't much money due to Smallie's treatment, but we never complained, we never demanded things. We knew and understood the situations of the house and the struggles Mum and Dad were facing.

But even though times were rough, my parents never made anything less for us, for their kids. When Smallie was taken for his first operation, it was during Christmas time in 2014 (if I'm not mistaken; you might have to check the date on that one). Mum went along with Smallie and Shaun. Dad was sailing at that time. Nobody really came for help or support; it was just Mum and us. I stayed alone in the house during that time because I was in the Tenth Grade, and someone had to stay back to take care of the house.

Shaun and I had to grow up much earlier, and I think it wasn't a bad thing at all because we learnt to take responsibility, to make the best of what we have, to be strong. I still remember sometimes Dad would give Shaun and me advice on life, which I never really understood back then. But slowly, I realised what he meant and what he was trying to tell us.

"My dad always used to say, "LIFE IS NEVER A BED OF ROSES!""

ᐯᐯᐯ